W9-AMN-107
3 4028 07578 0842
HARRIS COUNTY PUBLIC LIBRARY

JPIC Clifto
Clifton-Brown, Holly
Annie Hoot and the Knitting
extravaganza
DISCARD
$16.95
ocn473650409
1st American ed   11/24/2010

This book is for my Granny Japan.

Thank you Mum, Dad, Emma, Laura, Ashley, Bex, and Ben.

First American edition published in 2010 by Andersen Press USA, an imprint of Andersen Press Ltd.
www.andersenpressusa.com
First published in Great Britain in 2010 by Andersen Press Ltd., 20 Vauxhall Bridge Road, London SW1V 2SA.
Published in Australia by Random House Australia Pty., Level 3, 100 Pacific Highway, North Sydney, NSW 2060.
Copyright © Holly Clifton-Brown, 2010.

The author and the artist assert the moral right to be identified as author and artist of this work.
All rights reserved. No part of this book may be reproduced, stored in a retrieval system, or transmitted in any
form or by any means—electronic, mechanical, photocopying, recording, or otherwise—without the prior written
permission of Andersen Press Ltd., except for the inclusion of brief quotations in an acknowledged review.

Distributed in the United States and Canada by
Lerner Publishing Group, Inc.
241 First Avenue North
Minneapolis, MN 55401 U.S.A.
www.lernerbooks.com

Color separated in Switzerland by Photolitho AG, Zürich. Printed and bound in Singapore by Tien Wah Press.
Holly Clifton-Brown has used watercolor in this book.
Library Cataloging-in-Publication Data available.
ISBN 978-0-7613-6444-3
1 – TWP – 1/1/2010

Annie Hoot
and the
Knitting Extravaganza

Holly Clifton-Brown

ANDERSEN PRESS USA

Annie Hoot was a kind but scatterbrained little owl. She lived in a tree house deep in the woods.

She was always coming up with new ideas for things to do, and her latest craze was knitting.

She knitted morning, noon, and night. She knitted sweaters, socks, hats, and scarves.

She knitted squares and stripes and spots and stars. In fact, she knitted just about anything you could think of!

Sadly,
the other
owls wouldn't wear
the clothes that
Annie knitted for them.
"They are too bright," they said.
"We don't want to look different
from the other owls."
Annie decided to find
some animals who
would want her
nifty knitwear.
She knitted
herself a . . .

hot air balloon,

and off she sailed.

The wind blew her all the way to . . .

the rain forest.

It was a bit too wet for Annie's liking, but the treetops were full of the most exquisite birds she had ever seen.

"Don't worry," she told them. "I'll knit you something to keep you dry."

The birds were delighted, but
as the rain poured down, the
knitted umbrellas sagged.
"We know who would really love your
knitting, Annie," the birds said.

"The animals on the African plains get chilly at night." So Annie knitted herself a . . .

sail for a little wooden boat, and
she sailed across the sea.

She trekked up and down the dunes, and at last, she arrived on the plains.

"I've come to knit you some lovely warm clothes to keep you snug at night," she told the animals.

She knitted long, stripy scarves for the giraffes, an enormous, snazzy sweater for the elephant, and a huge hat for the big cat. But when the sun came up, the animals found the clothes too hot.

"Our friends at the North Pole would love your knitting, Annie. It's cold all the time there," they said. So Annie knitted herself a . . .

parachute and glided over the mountains.

She skidded over

the icebergs and . . .

bumped into a polar bear's shivering bottom.

The arctic animals huddled 'round.
"I've come to knit you wonderful and warm things,"
Annie explained to them.

She knitted polka~dot pullovers for the penguins, a pair of dazzling diamond~patterned pajamas for the polar bear, and a wonderful woolly waistcoat for the walrus!

"Thank you, Annie. What cozy and colorful gifts!" they said. "Now we will be snug all the time!"

Annie was pleased that at last she had found
some animals who really needed her knitting.

But she had run out of yarn and she missed her
tree house and the other owls, so she decided
to fly all the way home.

"Hoot, hoot, hooray!

Annie's home!" the owls cried.

"We missed you so much, Annie, that we started wearing your nifty knitwear."

Annie was happy to be home and delighted to know her friends now loved her gifts.

"Annie, Annie," they cried.

"Please teach us to knit too."

And so Annie did.

And that very afternoon, as they all knitted happily together, she told them about her travels and the amazing animals that she had met all around the world.

Harris County Public Library
Houston, Texas